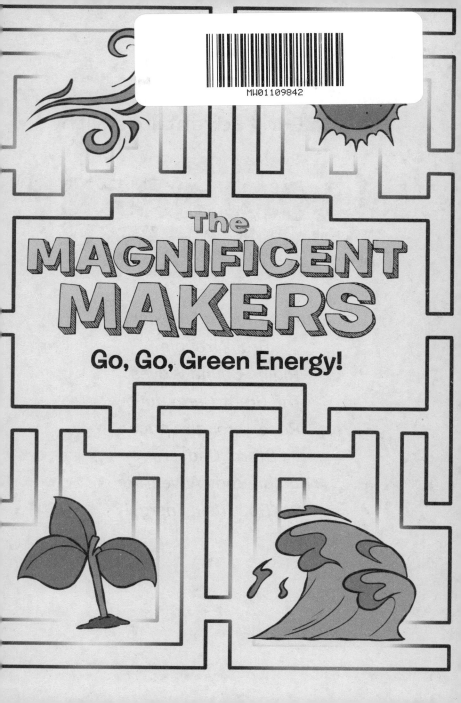

The MAGNIFICENT MAKERS

Go, Go, Green Energy!

Go on more
a-MAZE-ing adventures with

The
MAGNIFICENT
MAKERS

How to Test a Friendship
Brain Trouble
Riding Sound Waves
The Great Germ Hunt
Race Through Space
Storm Chasers
Human Body Adventure
Go, Go, Green Energy!

The MAGNIFICENT MAKERS

Go, Go, Green Energy!

by Theanne Griffith
illustrated by Leo Trinidad

A STEPPING STONE BOOK™
Random House 🏠 New York

For Charlie:
Be bold, be brave, & measure up!!

Sale of this book without a front cover may be unauthorized. If the book is coverless, it may have been reported to the publisher as "unsold or destroyed" and neither the author nor the publisher may have received payment for it.

This is a work of fiction. Names, characters, places, and incidents either are the product of the author's imagination or are used fictitiously. Any resemblance to actual persons, living or dead, events, or locales is entirely coincidental.

Text copyright © 2024 by Theanne Griffith
Cover art copyright © 2024 by Reginald Brown
Interior illustrations by Leo Trinidad, inspired by the work of Reginald Brown

All rights reserved. Published in the United States by Random House Children's Books, a division of Penguin Random House LLC, New York.

Random House and the colophon are registered trademarks and A Stepping Stone Book and the colophon are trademarks of Penguin Random House LLC.

Visit us on the Web!
rhcbooks.com

Educators and librarians, for a variety of teaching tools, visit us at RHTeachersLibrarians.com

Library of Congress Cataloging-in-Publication Data is available upon request.
ISBN 978-0-593-70340-3 (trade)—ISBN 978-0-593-70341-0 (lib. bdg.)—
ISBN 978-0-593-70342-7 (ebook)

Printed in the United States of America
10 9 8 7 6 5 4 3 2 1

First Edition

This book has been officially leveled by using
the F&P Text Level Gradient™ Leveling System.

Random House Children's Books supports the
First Amendment and celebrates the right to read.

Penguin Random House LLC supports copyright. Copyright fuels creativity, encourages diverse voices, promotes free speech, and creates a vibrant culture. Thank you for buying an authorized edition of this book and for complying with copyright laws by not reproducing, scanning, or distributing any part in any form without permission. You are supporting writers and allowing Penguin Random House to publish books for every reader.

For my little-big girl, Violeta.
I love you so much.
—T.G.

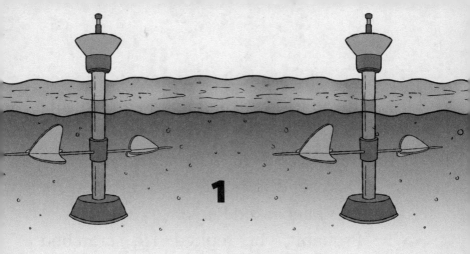

"**W**hew!" Violet wiped drops of sweat from her forehead. "Is it just me, or is it super hot today?" She grabbed her wild, curly hair and lifted it off her neck.

Pablo nodded and fanned himself with his hand. "I should've worn a T-shirt." He rolled up his sleeves.

The two best friends were on a field trip with their third-grade classmates from Newburg Elementary. It was Earth Day, and they were getting ready to tour the brand-new Environmental Science

Center. The students were excited to see what was inside. They had been waiting for a while already, and everyone was getting restless.

"Do you think actual scientists work here?" Violet asked Pablo.

"Probably," he replied. He scratched his cheek. "It is a science center after all. Hopefully we can go in soon and find out." He kept fanning his face.

Violet and Pablo became best friends in first grade when Pablo moved to Newburg from Puerto Rico. They had a lot in common and did just about everything together. They loved soccer and always played on the same team during recess. Their favorite color was red, and their favorite food was pickles. Especially the fried pickles they ate at the Newburg County Fair. They both also loved science.

Violet wanted to help people by becoming a scientist who studies different types of diseases. She was going to be the boss of her own laboratory one day. Pablo loved everything about space. He dreamt of becoming an astronaut and launching rockets when he grew up. Maybe he would be the first astronaut to meet an alien!

"Real scientists *do* work here!" their classmate Garry said.

The two best friends turned around.

"Really?" asked Violet, excited. "How do you know?"

"Well, my parents are two of the scientists who helped create this center," Garry replied.

"Your parents are *real* scientists!" Pablo exclaimed. His eyes grew wide.

"You're so lucky!" said Violet with her

hands on her cheeks. "What kind of scientists are they? Do you have a lab in your house? Do you get to do experiments with them? Do they work here?" she asked, barely breathing between questions.

"I *wish* we had a lab at our house!" Garry giggled. Then he continued, "My parents don't work here. They work at the Newburg College. That's where their labs are. They study how to make solar panels better at turning light from the sun into electricity."

Pablo's eyes grew even wider. "*Whoa,* that sounds hard."

Garry laughed again and shrugged.

Before Violet could ask more questions, Mr. Eng passed by with plastic water bottles in his hands. "They are almost ready for us," he said. "I brought these from the bus for you all." He handed one each to Violet and Pablo. They opened them and started gulping down the cool water.

"Here you go, Garry," said Mr. Eng, holding out a bottle.

Garry smiled and shook his head. "No thanks. I don't like to use plastic."

"Are you sure?" Mr. Eng asked. "It's pretty hot out here."

"I'm sure," replied Garry.

"Okay then." Mr. Eng continued passing out bottles to the other students in line.

"What's wrong with plastic?" asked Pablo. "I thought it was okay to use as long as you recycle it."

Violet nodded, her mouth full of water.

"Recycling is good," said Garry. "But just like a trash dump, recycling plants produce pollution."

"Really?" asked Violet.

"Really," Garry repeated. "I have a reusable water bottle, but I forgot it at home today."

Violet looked at the plastic bottle in her hand and frowned. *I didn't know plastic was so bad,* she thought. Just then, the doors to the Environmental Science Center opened.

"Welcome, students!" A woman with curly red hair and freckles smiled as she held the door open with her foot. "Sorry to keep you waiting. My name is Allie, and I will be your guide today. Come on in!"

2

The Environmental Science Center was bigger on the inside than it looked from the outside. The main floor was filled with different exhibits. Nearby, a row of model windmills were lined up behind a rope. Some seemed as if they were from fairy tales, and others were like the ones that dotted the hills of Newburg. Against the back wall was a long wave pool with a machine that looked like an upside-down windmill and measured the energy created by the waves. On the opposite side was an exhibit about solar panels.

"Feel free to look around for a bit!" Allie hollered over the voices of the excited students. "Let's gather on the rug of the multimedia area in ten minutes." She pointed to a rainbow-colored rug in the far corner of the room that was sur-rounded by bookshelves and a row of computer workstations.

"That's the exhibit my parents helped build!" Garry pointed to the line of solar panels mounted on a wall.

"Let's go check it out!" said Violet. She grabbed Garry's and Pablo's hands and darted toward the display.

"Are these from your parents' lab?" asked Pablo. He pressed his face up against the display case holding several small black squares with lines on them.

"Yup! Well, some of them. They're called *solar cells*. Solar panels are made up of a bunch of solar cells that turn sunlight into electricity. That's their latest model." Garry pointed toward the far end of the display. "It can turn almost half of

the sunlight that hits it into electricity!" he explained.

"Is that a lot?" asked Violet.

"Oh yeah. That's *eight more times* the amount of electricity than this one could make." Garry hurried toward the other end of the display. He pointed and said, "That's one of the first solar cells ever made. It was invented about seventy years ago."

"Seventy years!" said Violet. "That's as old as my grandpa!"

The three friends laughed. Just then, Mr. Eng hollered from the center of the room, "Okay, students, it's time to join Allie on the rug."

Violet, Pablo, and Garry gathered in the multimedia corner with the rest of their classmates.

"I hope you had fun exploring!" said Allie with a smile as students sat down. "You'll have plenty of extra time to do more. But first I wanted to chat with you about our current exhibits. Did you notice anything that they all have in common?"

Pablo and Violet's friend Aria raised her hand. "They're all about things that make energy," she answered.

"That's correct!" said Allie. "The exhibits you'll find here today are all about energy. *Renewable* energy to be specific." She turned on one of the computers and flipped a switch on the wall. A slit opened in the ceiling and a screen began to lower from above as Allie opened a file on the computer. The image on the computer appeared for the class to see on the big screen. It read:

ENERGY! Where does it come from?

A **natural resource** is anything found in nature that can be used by other living things. We use energy from natural resources to make electricity!

Nonrenewable energy is created from resources that are available in limited amounts. They are also called *fossil fuels* because they formed millions of years ago from dead plants and animals. These resources are not easily replaced by nature.

- Coal, oil, and natural gas are natural resources used to make nonrenewable energy.

Renewable energy is energy created from resources that are replaced by nature. Renewable energy sources are easily replaced by nature. They could last us thousands (or maybe even millions!) of years.

- Wind, sunlight, and moving water are renewable energy sources.

"How we make energy has important consequences for our environment," Allie explained. "We burn fossil fuels to make energy, but that creates a lot of pollution. Chemicals are released into the air and water, which is bad for the environment."

Violet raised her hand. "Is clean energy the same thing as renewable energy?" she asked.

"Yes!" responded Allie. "Energy from renewable resources is often called *clean* or *green* energy because it causes little to no pollution."

A few more hands shot into the air. As Allie continued answering students' questions, Violet's mind began to wander. She knew it was important not to waste electricity. But she never thought too much about where her electricity came from. Or the effects wasting electricity had on the environment. She remembered all the times she forgot to turn off the lights in rooms after she left. And how she liked to crank up the heat during the winter, so she didn't have to wear long pajamas to bed. She got a funny feeling in her stomach. When she finally looked back up, she gasped. The screen no longer showed Allie's slide. There was a riddle instead!

What is going on? Violet thought.

Allie didn't seem to notice. Neither did Mr. Eng or the rest of her classmates. Her eyes darted to Pablo. His mouth was wide open.

"Are you seeing what I'm seeing?" Violet whispered.

"I think so," Pablo said in an unsure voice.

"So . . . I'm not the only one who is confused?" asked Garry.

The two best friends looked at their classmate in surprise.

Pablo smiled. "Do you like adventure, Garry?"

3

Violet and Pablo told Garry what was happening. They explained how they needed to solve the riddle on the screen to open a portal that would transport them to the Maker Maze.

"The Maker Maze is like a huge, super-powered, magical lab," said Pablo.

"Dr. Crisp is the scientist in charge," added Violet. "She has this book, the Maker Manual. It designs a science challenge for us. Each challenge has three levels."

"And *we* get to choose the topic!" said Pablo.

"I knew today would be fun. But I didn't expect it to be *this* fun!" replied Garry in a happy but hushed voice.

"We also get these cool watches that keep track of time," continued Pablo. "We have one hundred twenty Maker Minutes to complete all three levels. If we don't finish in time, we can't go back. And trust me, you'll want to go back."

"The watches also shoot lasers and holograms!" said Violet, a little *too* loudly.

Mr. Eng looked toward the trio of friends. He removed a pencil from behind his ear and put it in front of his lips. They needed to stay quiet.

19

"Sorry," Violet mouthed to Mr. Eng. Then she whispered, "I wonder why no one else can see the riddle."

"No idea," said Pablo, "but let's solve it!"

Violet, Pablo, and Garry read the screen silently:

WE POWER OUR PLANET WITH ELECTRICITY,
WHICH WE MAKE FROM ENERGY.
MOST OF OUR ENERGY COMES FROM
_____.
BUT WITH THEM WE MUST TAKE CARE.
IF WE ARE TOO WASTEFUL,
WE WILL HAVE NONE LEFT TO SPARE!
WE MUST ALSO USE THEM WISELY,
BECAUSE THEY CAN _____ THE AIR!
_____ IS A BETTER CHOICE TO CHOOSE.

OUR _____ ARE GIFTS,
ONES WE CAN'T AFFORD TO LOSE.

Violet bit her lip. "This is a little tricky. . . ."

"Maybe the first one is fossil fuels?" Garry suggested. "That is where most of the energy we use comes from."

"If the first blank is *fossil fuels,* then I bet the second one is *pollute,*" Pablo whispered.

Violet nodded. "Renewable energy is a better choice than something that pollutes the air," she added. "I think that's the third blank."

"So . . . what's the last one?" asked Pablo, scratching his cheek.

The trio sat and thought for a while. Finally, Garry said, "Natural resources?"

Allie was still speaking as the rug beneath the students started to vibrate. So did the large screen and computer. Books trembled and began to fall from the bookshelves. Violet, Pablo, and Garry bounced up and down.

Garry grabbed Pablo's arm. "Is this an earthquake?" he squeaked. "Why doesn't anyone else notice the whole building is shaking?"

"Just hold on!" Pablo replied. "It will be over soon."

BOOM! SNAP! WHIZ! ZAP!

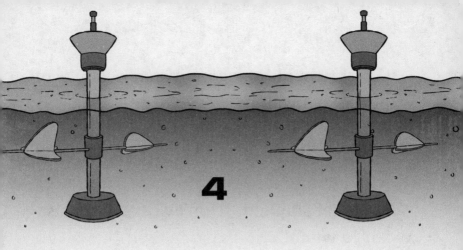

4

Everything was suddenly calm and quiet. Everyone was frozen in place. Allie was pointing at the screen. Students still had their hands raised. Mr. Eng was in the back with a serious look on his face.

"What just happened?" asked Garry.

"The portal opened. Now we need to find it," answered Violet.

"Over there!" Pablo pointed toward the entrance.

The trio ran to the windmill display.

One of them was glowing in a circle of purple light.

"That's the portal?" asked Garry. "It looks like the house Hansel and Gretel walked into. . . . "

Violet laughed. "Don't worry; Dr. Crisp isn't a witch!"

Garry leaned in to inspect the windmill. It was white with a little red door.

BIZZAP!

Garry giggled. "That tickled. How are we going to—" He felt a tug on his arm. "Aaaaaaaaah!" he shouted.

BIZZAP!

The tiny red door opened, and he was sucked through.

Violet grabbed Pablo's hand. "Let's go get him."

BIZZAP!

They landed feetfirst on the main floor of the Maker Maze next to Garry.

Garry's eyebrows were raised and his mouth was open. "That was kind of weird," he said finally. "But this is really . . . amazing."

Garry stared in wonder at all the gadgets around him. The room had long lab tables covered with flasks, which were filled with colorful bubbling liquid, and different kinds of strange plants. There were huge jars filled with even stranger bugs. One looked like a firefly, but its head glowed instead of its butt. A robot zoomed by, holding a zero gravity chamber on its head. Garry walked over to a large microscope and peeked down a long hallway lined with doors.

"Do we go through one of those?" he asked, slightly nervous.

"You bet your pipette!" sounded a voice from behind.

"Dr. Crisp!" cheered Violet and Pablo.

The three friends turned to face a tall woman with wild rainbow hair who was wearing a white lab coat and purple pants. A glittery golden lab book was tucked under her arm.

"Glad you could join us today, Garry!" said Dr. Crisp.

Garry blinked several times. "You know my name?"

Dr. Crisp held the shiny book in front of the Makers. "Yup! And I also know you all are ready for *adventure*!" She winked.

Garry's eyebrows reached even farther up his forehead as he tilted his head to look at Violet and Pablo. They just giggled.

Then Dr. Crisp opened the Maker Manual to a page with a giant question mark on it. "And today's science topic is . . . ?"

"How about renewable energy?" said Pablo.

Garry's expression changed from confused to excited. "Yeah!" he and Violet cheered.

The pages of the Maker Manual began to turn at lightning speed. They suddenly stopped on a page that read:

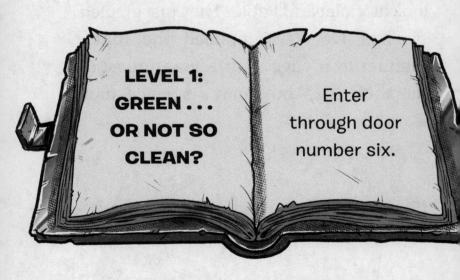

LEVEL 1: GREEN . . . OR NOT SO CLEAN?

Enter through door number six.

Dr. Crisp closed the book and tucked it inside a backpack sitting on one of the lab tables.

Violet glanced at all the different pieces of equipment that hummed with the energy that powered them. "The Maker Maze must use a lot of electricity," said Violet.

"Yes, indeed! The power of science relies on a lot of . . . *power*! But we are one hundred percent *clean* and *green* in the Maker Maze!" Dr. Crisp spread her arms and said, "All the science stuff you see is powered by renewable energy sources. Which you will learn about soon!" Dr. Crisp winked. Then she clapped her hands and shouted, "Magnificent Maker Watches ready to roll?"

Garry gazed down at his wrist, and the

smile on his face grew. "Yes!" he cheered, raising his hand.

"Me too!" added Pablo.

Violet lifted her wrist. But that funny feeling returned to her tummy. She remembered her tablet was still plugged in to an outlet in her room. Her dad always told her to unplug it when the battery was charged to save electricity. But today she forgot. *Is that being wasteful? How much pollution does charging a tablet create?* Her thoughts felt like pesky flies.

Pablo tapped Violet on the shoulder. "Are you okay?"

Violet ignored the uneasy feeling in her stomach. "Yeah. Let's go!"

The Makers followed as Dr. Crisp galloped down the never-ending hallway toward door number six.

∿

The room was large, white, and empty. But not for long . . .

Dr. Crisp pressed a button on the side of her watch and shouted, "Maker Maze, activate Energy Sources!"

A blast of bright purple light filled the room. Violet, Pablo, and Garry shielded their eyes. When the light faded, they noticed a line of five holograms floating on the left side of the room. On the right side, the words *renewable* and *nonrenewable* floated in the air.

"All righty, Makers. Listen up!" Dr.

Crisp called out between her two cupped hands. "In this level, you all will need to work together to decide whether the holograms on your left are sources of renewable or nonrenewable energy."

Dr. Crisp walked over toward the hologram of a sun and pressed a button on the side of her watch. A laser shot out!

BIZZAP!

"All you have to do is use your watch to scan the hologram, then drag it under the right category," she explained. She pointed back to the floating words on the other side of the room.

"Whoa," said Garry. "These watches *are* fancy!"

Dr. Crisp turned off her laser and blew a puff of air on her nails. She polished them on her lab coat and said, "That's how we do things in the Maker Maze!" Then she raised both arms and lowered them quickly.

"Ready, set, SORT!"

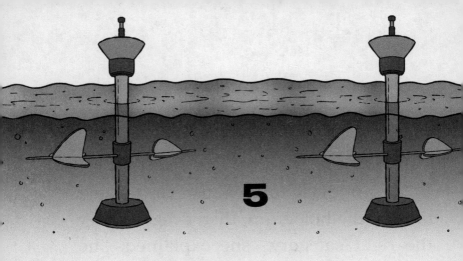

5

Violet, Pablo, and Garry walked toward the line of holograms. Next to the sun was a pile of coal, then a crashing wave, followed by a well with bubbling oil at the bottom. The last one looked empty.

Violet shouted back to Dr. Crisp. "I think this one is broken!"

"I would think again!" replied Dr. Crisp. She put her hands behind her back and started whistling.

Pablo walked over to inspect it. A strong breeze blew over his face. He turned back to Violet and Garry. "It's not broken. It's the wind!" he said excitedly.

"That's definitely a renewable energy source!" said Garry.

"Want to scan it?" asked Violet. She nudged Garry a few times in his side.

"Yes, please!" he responded. Garry walked over to the last hologram and felt a gust of wind. He found the same button on his watch that Dr. Crisp used to scan the sun.

BIZZAP!

Garry pointed the laser toward the hologram. Wind filled the room as he moved it under the word *renewable.*

Dr. Crisp's wild rainbow hair blew all

over the place. She grabbed a handheld pirate's telescope from her lab coat pocket and said, "Ahoy, mateys! I think a storm's a coming in!"

The Makers giggled.

RING, DING, DONG!

Garry looked up and around the room. "What was that?" he asked as he ran back over to join Violet and Pablo.

"That's the Maker Maze jingle. It goes off every time we get something right during the challenge," Violet explained.

"Which one should we do next?" asked Pablo

"How about coal?" Garry suggested. "It's a fossil fuel."

Violet and Pablo nodded. Violet scanned the coal and dragged it under the word *nonrenewable*.

RING, DING, DONG!

It was Pablo's turn. He scanned the oil. The Makers agreed it was also a non-renewable source of energy. Then Violet scanned the sun and placed it under the word *renewable*.

RING, DING, DONG!

There was one hologram left.

"Is water renewable?" asked Pablo. "I've always been told not to waste water."

Dr. Crisp pretended to wash her armpits. "I like to keep my showers short!"

That sinking feeling returned to Violet's stomach. *I always take really long showers,* she thought. *How much water have I wasted?* She felt worried.

"Violet?" said Pablo. "Are you okay? You look . . . sad."

Violet hesitated, then stood up tall. "I'm fine. I was just . . . thinking."

Pablo squinted his eyes at his best friend. "Are you sure you're okay?"

"Yes," Violet insisted. "Actually, I have an idea." She walked closer to the hologram.

"This isn't just water. It's a wave," she said.

Pablo squinted. "But a wave is . . . water."

"Yeah. *Moving* water," Violet replied.

"Surf's up!" hollered Dr. Crisp. She pretended to ride a wave.

"Oooooooooh!" said Garry. "Just like the wind is moving air!"

"Exactly!" said Violet.

"Wait, what?" said Pablo. He was still confused.

"Wind is moving air. Waves are moving water," Violet explained. "Remember back at the Environmental Science Center? There was a wave pool! And it had an upside-down windmill in it. I think it was taking the energy from the waves and turning it into electricity."

"That upside-down windmill is a turbine!" added Garry. "And it's called tidal energy. It's renewable. As long as there is water in our oceans, we will have waves that we can get energy from."

Garry shot out a laser from his watch and scanned the wave hologram. He placed it next to the sun and wind holograms.

RING, DING, DONG!

"We did it!" cheered the Makers.

"You all are *electrifying*!" cheered Dr. Crisp.

"And we have ninety-five Maker Minutes left!" said Pablo, holding his watch in the air. "We're not wasting time!"

"And that's a good thing! Maker Minutes are *not* renewable!" added Dr. Crisp.

Garry and Pablo giggled. Violet gave a small smile. But thoughts of the lights she didn't turn off, the tablet she left plugged in, and her long showers bounced around in her head. What else did she do that wasted energy?

Dr. Crisp grabbed her backpack and removed the Maker Manual. "Now let's find out what's next on our energy adventure!"

The glittery golden book snapped open. The pages fluttered until they landed on one that read:

LEVEL 2: DID SOMEONE SAY *PIZZA*?

Enter through door number twenty-three.

"Twenty-three!" Violet repeated. "Can we catch a ride from one of the robots?"

Dr. Crisp laughed. "Not this time." She closed the book, tossed it back into her bag, and ran out of door number six.

"But I'm sure you Makers have the *energy*!" Her voice echoed down the never-ending hallway.

Violet, Pablo, and Garry raced after her.

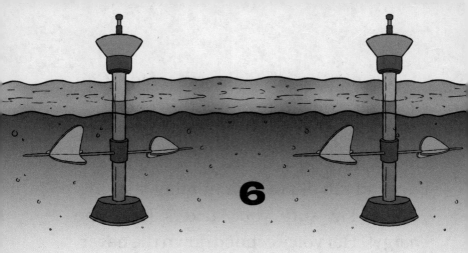

6

The Makers stood in the middle of a dry and dusty desert. Giant red rocks and tall green cacti surrounded them.

"And I thought it was hot back in Newburg," said Violet, fanning herself.

"Where are we?" asked Garry.

"In the Maker Maze!" responded Dr. Crisp.

"But this isn't a lab." Garry looked over his shoulders.

Pablo shielded his eyes from the

glaring sun. "The Maze can clone any place in the world!"

"You bet your bottom beaker!" Dr. Crisp tapped the screen of her watch three times and swiped left. The dry desert slid away. They were now standing in the middle of a large white room.

Garry's mouth dropped open. "Can I take my watch home?"

"Sorry! What's *made* in the Maker Maze *stays* in the Maker Maze," replied Dr. Crisp. She tapped her watch three more times and swiped right. The desert slid back into view. "All righty, Makers. It's time for my favorite part of each challenge. You've learned a bit about renewable energy. Now it's time to watch it work!"

Violet tapped the tips of her fingers

together. "What are we going to build?" she asked.

"An oven!" Dr. Crisp jumped into the air and clicked her heels.

The Makers exchanged confused looks.

"An oven?" repeated Pablo.

"Yup! A pizza oven!" Dr. Crisp opened her backpack and pulled out a pizza box.

"Okay, now I'm *really* confused," said Pablo.

Dr. Crisp kept removing supplies. She pulled out some pencils, a ruler, glue, a piece of black paper, scissors, aluminum foil, plastic wrap, and thick tape.

"That bag sure can hold a lot," said Garry, rubbing the back of his head.

Violet smiled. "That's nothing. It can hold a boat-sized plastic bottle!" Violet replied. But then she thought about what Garry had said outside the Environmental

Science Center. *We're not supposed to use plastic,* she remembered. She couldn't shake that nervous feeling. Her tummy began to turn again.

"Okay, Makers. Listen up!" said Dr. Crisp. "In the first part of this level, you will need to make a solar pizza box oven." She opened the Maker Manual and pointed to a list of instructions.

"Then you will have to figure out how it works!" She snapped the book shut. "On your mark, get set, MAKE!"

Violet, Pablo, and Garry huddled around the glittery book.

"First, we need to cut a big square out of the top," said Violet. She ignored her nervous stomach and grabbed the pair of scissors.

"We should probably use the ruler and pencil to draw the square," added Garry.

Violet nodded and passed the supplies to him. He began tracing. When he was finished, she cut out the square carefully.

"Uh-oh," said Pablo. "We weren't supposed to cut out the whole square. It's supposed to be like a flap."

"Oh yeah," said Garry, looking over the instructions again, "we shouldn't have cut along the back side of the square."

Violet sighed. "We're being so waste-ful." She crossed her arms and looked at the dusty ground.

"It was just a mistake," said Garry. "We can fix it!" He grabbed the tape and taped the back end of the cut-out square to the pizza box. He lifted and lowered. "See! Good as new."

"Okay," Violet mumbled.

"Now we need to cover the bottom of the flap and the inside of the box with aluminum foil," said Pablo. He grabbed the roll. "Want to help me?" He smiled at Violet.

"Sure," she replied.

Pablo cut out a piece of foil that was a little larger than the flap. Violet placed the sheet of foil on the underside of the flap and folded the edges over the top. Then Garry glued the edges down to keep them in place.

"Next, we need to tape plastic wrap over the opening," said Pablo. He pointed under the top flap.

"Plastic? I thought we shouldn't use plastic," said Violet. She felt nervous again. "Can we use something else instead?"

"Sometimes we have to use plastic,"

replied Garry. "My parents use plastic in their labs. You just need to be mindful about it!"

"Do you want to cut it out?" asked Pablo.

"It's all right," said Garry. "Go ahead."

Violet nodded as she said, "Sure."

She reached for the plastic wrap and scissors. The first piece she cut was too small. "Sorry. I didn't want to use too much."

She tried again. This time the piece was the right size. But when she tried to tape it down, the edges got stuck to each other. She tried to straighten it out, but it was too sticky.

"I'm so sorry," she said again. Her voice cracked. Her hands started to shake. *Don't be wasteful,* she thought.

Pablo rubbed her shoulder. "It's fine. Just relax and try again. You got this!"

She cut out another piece. As she grabbed the tape, a gust of wind blew across the desert. The piece of plastic wrap flew through the air.

Violet started breathing faster and faster. She couldn't hold it in anymore. She couldn't ignore the thoughts flooding her mind.

"Noooooooo!" she shouted into the sky.

7

"**W**hat's the matter, Violet?" asked Garry, worried.

Violet hugged her tummy. "I feel . . . ," she began, "nervous."

"About what?" replied Pablo. He looked at his watch. "We aren't even running out of time like we usually do."

Dr. Crisp rushed over to join them. "What's cooking, Makers?"

"Not pizza." Violet sighed. "I feel bad, Dr. Crisp. It seems like everything I do is wasteful and hurting the planet."

Dr. Crisp pulled a pencil from behind her ear and rubbed her chin. "Why is that?"

"How are you hurting the planet?" added Pablo.

"Well, I forgot to unplug my tablet this morning, even though it was already charged. I don't always remember to turn off the lights when I leave the room," said Violet. "Even though my dad reminds me. And I don't like to be cold. So I crank up the heat kind of high in the winter. And I also take long showers. But I didn't know! I promise I didn't!"

"Oh, Violet," said Dr. Crisp. "Taking care of our planet is everyone's job. Not just yours."

Violet didn't seem to hear her. "I didn't know that making electricity polluted the planet. And now it's all I can think about."

"Violet, it's good to think about these things," Garry said softly. "It means you care. But we all need to do better. Even me."

"You?" Violet repeated.

"Of course!" Garry replied. Then he whispered, "Can I tell you a secret?"

Violet nodded and leaned in to listen. So did Pablo and Dr. Crisp.

"I used to be scared of the dark, so I'd sleep with the light on." Garry giggled. "It feels kind of silly to say now."

"Really? You used to leave the light on? *All* night?" Violet couldn't believe it.

"Yup. Until this year. My parents didn't like it because it was wasteful. But I was so scared that they let me do it."

Dr. Crisp bent down toward Violet. "If you're worried about something, it's good to talk about it. When worries build up

inside, they make us feel not so good," she explained.

"Yeah, that makes sense," Violet replied. "I think I understand better now. How we create energy matters. And some ways are definitely better for our planet than others." Then she cracked a smile. "It's pretty fun learning about renewable energy! Maybe I'll be like Garry's parents when I grow up . . . and run a planet-saving clean, green energy lab!"

"That sounds awesome!" cheered Garry. "Can I work with you?"

"Maybe you'll discover a new clean energy source that we can use to launch my rocket into space!" added Pablo.

The Makers laughed.

"Go, go, green energy!" said Dr. Crisp. She stood back up. "Thanks for trusting us and sharing what worried you, Violet."

"Thanks for listening." Violet gave Dr. Crisp a hug. Then she took a deep breath and turned to Garry and Pablo. "Let's get back to oven building."

Violet carefully cut out a piece of plastic wrap and placed it over the cut-out portion of the pizza box lid. Garry and Pablo helped her tape it in place. Then they glued foil to cover the bottom of the box. They also glued foil to the inside of the lid, making sure to go around the plastic-covered opening. When they were finished, the entire inside of the pizza box was covered in foil.

"Now we just need to cut out a sheet of black paper and glue it to the bottom," said Pablo.

Garry grabbed the scissors and a piece of black construction paper. "Here?" he asked.

"Looks good to me!" replied Violet.

To finish, the Makers propped up the flap using a pencil taped to the side of the pizza box.

RING, DING, DONG!

"Yes!" Violet, Pablo, and Garry celebrated. They gave one another high fives.

"That was a *clean* finish, Makers! But remember, the level isn't over yet," said Dr. Crisp. She reached for her backpack. After a few seconds, she carefully pulled out a small, uncooked pickle pizza! She held it in the palm of her hand.

"PICKLE PIZZA!" Violet and Pablo shouted.

Garry tilted his head. "Wait. Are we really baking?"

Pablo looked down at his watch. "I hope we have time to eat it! We only have fifty Maker Minutes left!" he said.

50 min. left

"Let's see how quickly you can *cook up* some good ideas!" Dr. Crisp replied. She cupped her hands around her mouth and shouted, "Ready, set, THINK!"

8

The Makers set the pizza on top of the black piece of construction paper, under the plastic wrap covering. They propped up the aluminum-foil covered flap with the pencil. Then they waited.

Pablo checked his watch again nervously. "How long is this supposed to take?"

Garry shrugged. "It's pretty small, but it could take a while."

"We don't have to wait for the pizza to finish cooking," explained Violet. "We just need to figure out how the oven turns sunlight into energy to cook the pizza."

Pablo scratched his cheek. "That's true. . . ."

They inspected the oven carefully.

"The solar cells my parents make trap sun energy," said Garry, thinking aloud. "They need to trap more heat than they lose."

"So something in our oven is trapping the energy from the sun. What do you think it is?" asked Pablo.

Garry looked closely. He was unsure.

Then Violet said, "Maybe it's the plastic wrap!" She got down on all fours and put her eyes in line with the oven. "It reminds me of a greenhouse roof! It traps heat so that plants can grow even when it's cold outside."

"I bet you're right!" Garry agreed.

"Okay, if plastic traps heat, what do you think the aluminum foil is for?" Violet continued.

They kept thinking as time ticked away.

Pablo took a deep breath. "We need to hurry!"

"We're trying!" Violet exclaimed.

"Wait!" shouted Garry. "Let me see

something." He moved the pizza box so the propped-open flap faced directly toward the sun.

"Ahhh!" cried Violet and Pablo, covering their faces with their hands. A strong beam of sunlight hit them in the eyes as Garry moved the box.

"Be careful!" Violet complained. "The sun bounced off the foil and—"

She suddenly stopped. She and Pablo lowered their hands and saw Garry kneeling next to the pizza box oven. "That's it!" Violet cheered.

"Yup! The foil reflects the sunlight! Straight into the oven!" said Garry, smiling. "You can even feel it!"

Garry waved his hand slowly under the foil-covered flap. Pablo and Violet did the same.

"Mmmmm. Toasty," said Pablo, laughing. Violet and Garry giggled.

"So maybe the oven works because the foil reflects sunlight into the box and the plastic wrap traps it there?" Violet continued.

They listened for the Maker Maze jingle. But the desert remained quiet.

"We must be missing something," said Pablo.

"What about the black construction paper?" asked Garry.

"It's just paper," replied Violet. "How could it help heat the oven?"

"Remember last summer when we went to the Newburg Fair?" Pablo asked Violet. "And you wore all black? And you were complaining the whole time?"

"Yeah . . . ," Violet began. "What does that have to do with anything?"

Pablo continued staring at Violet with wide eyes and a half-smile. "How did those black clothes make you *feel*?"

Violet paused and squinted her eyes. "They made me feel super . . . hot!"

"Exactly!" responded Pablo.

"That's because black materials absorb heat!" added Garry.

"Okay, we almost got this," said Violet, rubbing her hands together. "Step one: The sunlight reflects off the foil and bounces into the oven."

"Step two," Pablo continued. "The light gets absorbed by the black paper. That light energy turns into heat."

"Step three: The plastic wrap traps the energy! And BOOM! We have a solar oven!" Garry finished.

RING, DING, DONG!

"Way to go, Makers!" Dr. Crisp hustled over to the group. "We may have to rename this place the *Baker Maze*! Look at that pizza!"

The cheese was bubbling around thin green pickle slices.

"Whoa!" said Garry. "That only took, like, twenty minutes." He checked his watch. They had thirty Maker Minutes left.

"I want to eat that *soooo* badly!" Violet wiggled with excitement.

"We definitely don't waste anything in the Maker Maze!" replied Dr. Crisp. She tapped her watch three times and swiped right. The desert slid away. They were back in room twenty-three, and the pizza box oven sat on a long white lab table.

Dr. Crisp shouted into her watch. "Maker Maze, slice it up!"

The pizza box oven started to spin. It spun faster and faster until it nearly looked like a pizza tornado!

BOOM! SNAP! WHIZ! ZAP!

The oven suddenly stopped. The small pickle pizza was cut into three even pieces.

"Eat up!" said Dr. Crisp.

Violet and Pablo each grabbed a slice. Garry passed.

"No thanks." Garry shook his head. "I don't like pickles. Especially on pizza."

"You have no idea what you're missing," said Violet with her mouth full. "Dr. Crisp, you should try it!"

"Don't mind if I do!" She reached for the slice and took a big bite. The cheese stretched into a long strand as she pulled it away from her mouth. *"Magnificent!"* she said. As she went in for another bite, she fumbled the slice. Cheese and pickles spilled on her lab coat.

"Fiddle flasks!" Dr. Crisp said, wiping herself off. "Oh well, no time to cry over

spilled pizza. We have a challenge to finish! In twenty-five minutes!"

Violet and Pablo scarfed down their slices as Dr. Crisp grabbed the Maker Manual from her backpack. It opened to a page that read:

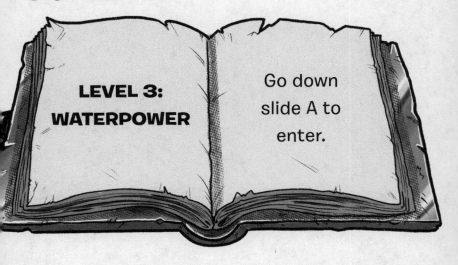

LEVEL 3: WATERPOWER

Go down slide A to enter.

"Slide A?" Garry repeated.

Dr. Crisp tossed the Maker Manual into her backpack and headed toward a small door at the back of the room. When she opened it, the Makers could see the top of a bright purple spiraling slide. Dr. Crisp sat down on the slide and raised both hands in the air.

"Follow *meeeeee!*" Her voice echoed as she disappeared into the darkness.

9

Violet, Pablo, and Garry landed one by one with a thud at the bottom of the slide. They got up and dusted themselves off. Dr. Crisp was standing at the other end of the room in front of a long purple curtain that covered the entire wall. She yanked hard on a rope, and the curtain slowly opened. Behind it hung a huge clear tub of water with a long tube sticking out of the front. The end of the tube rested on top of another clear tub that sat on the floor with a water wheel inside. It looked like a small Ferris wheel, but with little buckets instead of seats.

"Okay, Makers! Listen up!" Dr. Crisp shouted across the room. "In this final level, you are going to learn how we get energy from water."

"I hope this won't take too long." Pablo checked his watch. "We only have twenty minutes left!"

Dr. Crisp continued, "One person is going to scan the hanging tub with their watch. It will let water flow through the tube and into the tub on the floor to turn the water wheel. Let's just say it will make *sparks* fly!" She pointed to a red button on the floor next to her. "Then, you'll stomp on this to raise the tub. You'll repeat the same steps until you figure out how water can be used to make electricity."

"This is confusing," said Violet. "We just keep raising the tub and releasing water to spin the water wheel? How will that tell us anything?"

"I'm sure once you give it a try, some

sparks of your own will fly!" said Dr. Crisp. Then she shouted, "Ready, set, TEST!"

The Makers huddled to discuss the level.

"We need to move fast," said Pablo. "Who is going to scan the hanging tub?"

Garry volunteered. "I can!"

"Okay, I can stomp on the red button," said Pablo.

"And I'll watch to see what happens," added Violet.

They all assumed their positions. Garry pressed a button on the side of his watch and scanned the tub.

BIZZAP!

A stream of water flowed down the clear tube into the tub on the floor. The water wheel began to spin.

BIZZAP!

A small purple spark went off above the water wheel.

"Did you see that?" asked Violet.

"Yeah!" Pablo and Garry responded.

"Let's see what happens when the tub is higher." Pablo went over and stomped on the red button. The tub of water slowly raised.

"Wow! Look at that!" Garry pointed to the tube, which was growing longer as the tub raised. "I didn't even know that was possible!"

"There's a lot of science in the Maker Maze," said Dr. Crisp. "But there's a little bit of magic, too!" She winked.

Garry scanned the tub again, releasing more water.

BIZZAP!

"That spark was even bigger!" cheered

Violet. "I think that means the water wheel made more energy this time."

Pablo stomped on the red button again. The tub rose higher, and the tube continued to stretch. "I have an idea," Pablo said. "We don't have a lot of time. What if I just keep stomping on the button until the tub reaches the ceiling? Then we can see what happens when the tub is super low or super high."

"Sounds like a good idea to me!" said Violet.

Garry nodded. "Let's test it!"

Pablo stomped on the red button over and over. The tube connecting the tubs grew to nearly fifteen feet long!

"Okay, here goes nothing!" shouted Garry.

BIZZAP!

He scanned the tub. A rush of water flew down the clear tube. The water wheel spun much faster than before!

Suddenly, the Makers felt the floor start

to shake. The friends exchanged worried looks. Out of nowhere a huge purple firework went off above the spinning water wheel.

BOOM! SNAP! WHIZ! ZAP!

10

A purple glow lit up Violet's, Pablo's, and Garry's faces. The room was now still.

"That was HUGE!" said Violet.

"I was *not* expecting that," said Garry.

"Me either," added Pablo. "But it may have given us the answer we needed."

"I'm still a little confused," said Violet. She bit her lip. "Why did raising the tub make the water wheel create more energy? It's not like more water came out."

"No . . . ," said Pablo, smiling, "but it did come out faster."

"Faster," Garry repeated under his breath. He rested his chin in one hand and closed his eyes to think.

"It's just like in level one," Pablo continued. "Remember the wave? It's not the water itself that gives us energy. It's moving water."

"That's right!" said Violet. Then she paused. "But the water was always moving. Even when the tub was low, the water flowed onto the wheel."

"Yes, but when we raised the tub to the ceiling, the water moved way faster!" replied Garry. "That's how dams work, too. Dams trap water. And as the water builds up, the water level gets higher and higher. When the water is released, it falls through pipes. Kind of like that one!" Garry pointed to the clear tube. "And there are turbines at the bottom that spin as the water hits them. That's what turns all that energy into electricity!"

"Oooooooh! You're right!" cheered Pablo. "I can't believe I didn't think about that."

"I think we got it! Moving water creates energy. The faster the water is moving, the more energy it makes!" said Violet.

RING, DING, DONG!

Dr. Crisp hurried over to the Makers, making wave motions with her hands. "Way to go with the flow and figure that one out!"

"I didn't think we were going to make it!" said Pablo.

Just then, Dr Crisp's watch started to

flash purple. She held it in the air. "We haven't made it just yet! Three minutes until the portal closes!"

Dr. Crisp ran over to the end of the slide. Then she shouted into her watch, "Maker Maze, activate steps!"

Steps rose from the spiral slide, turning it into a spiral staircase.

Pablo grabbed his cheeks. "We're never going to make it up all those in time!"

"Just run!" Dr. Crisp yelled. She bolted up the purple stairs.

Violet, Pablo, and Garry ran behind her. They made it to the top, nearly out of breath.

"We're still in room twenty-three!" said Pablo. "We only have one minute left!"

"I could use a renewable energy source right about now," said Violet, breathing heavily and bent over with her hands on her knees.

Garry giggled. But Pablo said, "No time for jokes! We have to hustle!"

The trio and Dr. Crisp darted out of room twenty-three and down the never-ending hallway. The light from the portal was dimming as they finally reached the main lab.

"Hurry and jump!" Dr. Crisp pointed.

"Can we make it that high?" asked Garry, looking at the ceiling.

"We don't have time to think about it. Just JUMP!" shouted Pablo.

The Makers squatted and leaped into the air with all their might.

BIZZAP!

The trio tumbled onto the rug. A few seconds later, everyone else unfroze.

Allie continued answering students' questions as if no time had passed. "Yes! The solar panels on your roof are made up of solar cells like the ones we have on display," she said.

Then Allie paused. "What happened here?" she said. She bent down to collect fallen books from the floor. She shrugged. "Any more questions?"

Violet, Pablo, and Garry giggled quietly to themselves.

When Allie finished her presentation, the students were allowed to continue exploring the Environmental Science Center. The three friends decided to check out the wave pool to learn more about tidal energy.

"Did all of that really happen?" asked Garry as they walked toward the exhibit.

"Oh yeah," replied Pablo. "And if we're lucky, we will get to go back again!"

"Now all I want to do is find ways to save energy," said Violet. She started scanning the room with her eyes. "I don't think we need all these lights on. I bet the center could save a lot of energy if we turned some off. I also hope they don't have to fill the wave pool every day.

That would be a huge waste of water. And look! Someone left their phone plugged into the wall. Maybe I should unplug it."

The trio heard a gentle laugh behind them. It was Mr. Eng. "That's my phone. But you're right, Violet. It's probably charged by now. I should unplug it. I just wanted to check on you all to see how you were enjoying the field trip."

"We're having a blast!" Violet replied. Then she noticed something on Mr. Eng's chest. She squinted her eyes. "Mr. Eng, I think you have a piece of pickle on your shirt." She pointed.

"Oh . . . ummm . . . hmmm . . ." Mr. Eng fumbled his words. "Sorry, let me go clean myself up." He hurried toward the bathroom.

"That was strange," said Garry. Then he

scrunched up his face. "I still can't believe you two actually like pickle pizza."

"You don't know what you're missing!" said Pablo, laughing.

"Yeah!" Violet said. "Pickles are my favorite *green* energy source!"

Make your own creations!

≽ MAKE A PIZZA BOX OVEN! ≼

Always *make* carefully and with adult supervision!

MATERIALS

1 large, clean pizza box
  aluminum foil
  black construction paper
  black electrical tape (Packaging
    tape works, too!)
  box cutter, scissors,
    or utility knife*
  glue
  pen or pencil
  plastic wrap

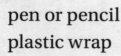

MATERIALS (CONT.)

ruler

sunlight and warm weather
(It should be 75°F/24°C or
warmer.)

wooden skewer or pencil

Please ask an adult for help when using sharp tools.

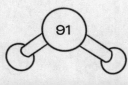

INSTRUCTIONS

1. Use your ruler and pen or pencil to draw a square on the top of the pizza box lid. There should be about one inch of space between the square and the edge of the lid.

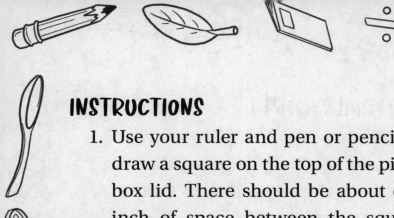

2. With the help of an adult, use a box cutter, scissors, or utility knife to *carefully* cut along three sides of the square. Do not cut along the side where the lid bends. You can use the ruler to help you cut straight.

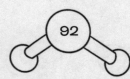

3. Fold the flap back along the side that is still attached. Glue aluminum foil to cover the bottom portion of the flap. You can fold the edges of the foil over 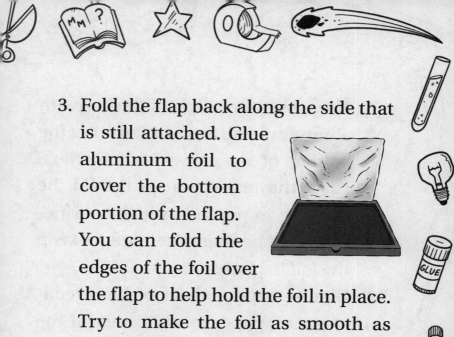 the flap to help hold the foil in place. Try to make the foil as smooth as possible.

4. Cover the square hole in the lid made by the flap with a layer of plastic wrap. Attach the plastic wrap to the opening's edges using black electrical tape or packaging tape. Make sure the square hole is completely sealed so heat cannot escape.

5. Now cover the inside of the box with aluminum foil. Start by covering the bottom of the box with foil. Next, cover the inside part of the lid. Be sure not to put foil over the plastic-covered opening. Use glue to keep the foil in place.

6. Glue or tape a sheet of black construction paper in the center of the bottom of the box, on top of the foil.

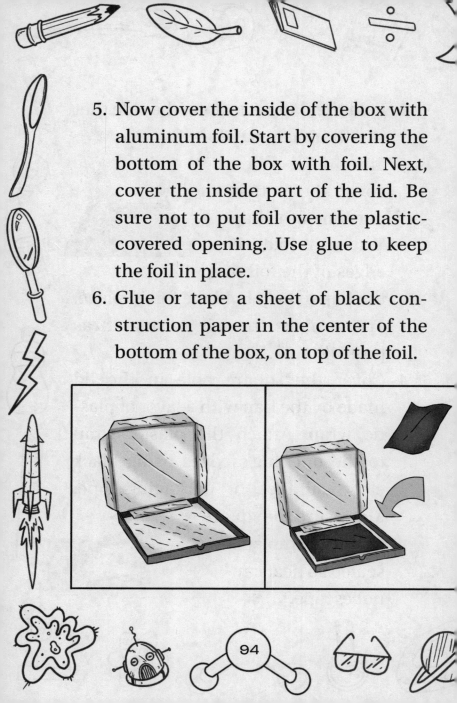

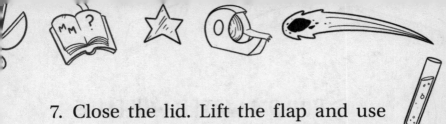

7. Close the lid. Lift the flap and use tape to secure a wooden skewer or pencil to prop the solar oven's lid up from the rest of the box. Now you're ready to start baking!

Your parent or guardian can share pictures and videos of your pizza box oven on social media using #MagnificentMakers.

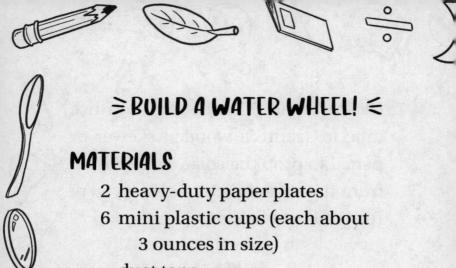

≥ BUILD A WATER WHEEL! ≤

MATERIALS

2 heavy-duty paper plates
6 mini plastic cups (each about
   3 ounces in size)
   duct tape
   wooden skewer or pencil

INSTRUCTIONS

1. Use the tip of your wooden skewer to *carefully* poke a hole through the center of each paper plate.

2. Turn one paper plate over so the bottom faces up. Then place the six plastic cups in a circle around the bottom of the plate. Try to evenly space out the cups. The bottom of the cups should all face the hole in the plate's center. The cups' tops should be close to the edge of the plate's inner ring.

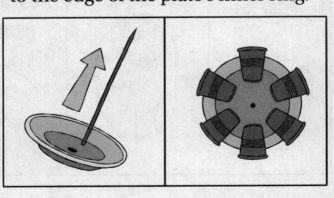

97

3. Secure each cup in place with a strip of duct tape.

4. Put the wooden skewer or pencil through the hole in the plate. Then stick the other plate onto the skewer. Both plate bottoms should face each other and touch the cups.

5. Use a small piece of duct tape to secure the top of each cup to the second plate.

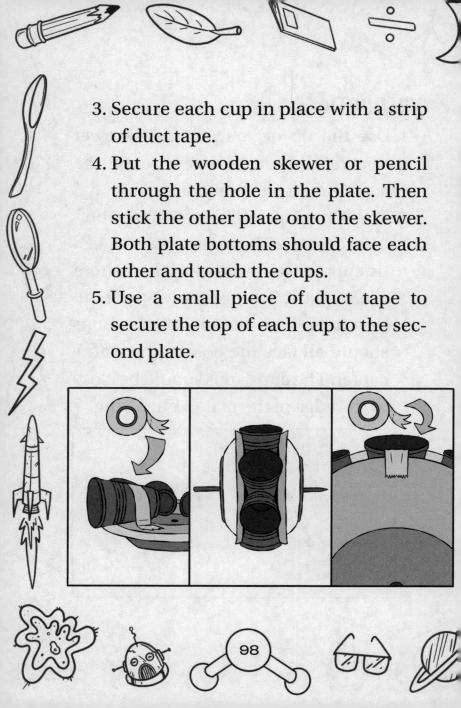

6. Test it! Take your water wheel to an empty bathtub, kitchen sink, or other water source. Turn on the water so it is running gently. Hold the ends of the skewer with both hands and place the wheel under the faucet.

7. The wheel should spin as the water hits the cups.

Your parent or guardian can share pictures and videos of your water wheel on social media using #MagnificentMakers.

Missing the
Maker Maze already?

Read on for a peek at the Magnificent
Makers' first adventure!

The Magnificent Makers: How to Test a Friendship
excerpt text copyright © 2020 by Theanne Griffith.
Cover art and excerpt illustrations copyright © 2020
by Reginald Brown.
Published by Random House Children's Books, a division of
Penguin Random House LLC, New York.

Pens and pencils? Check! Erasers? Check! Notebook? Check!

Pablo hopped in front of the mirror hanging on his bedroom door. The spaceship design on his new T-shirt matched the spaceships on his new sneakers. They were perfect for an astronaut-in-training. Awesome first-day-of-school outfit? Check!

Third grade, here I come! Pablo hurried downstairs. His parents were waiting for him by the front door.

"Are you ready?" asked his dad. He handed Pablo his spaceship lunch box.

"Yeah!" Pablo replied.

When Pablo and his parents arrived at Newburg Elementary, he saw his best friend. It was easy to spot Violet in a crowd. She was tall and had a head full of tightly coiled, dark brown curls.

Pablo and Violet had been best friends since he first moved to Newburg from Puerto Rico two years ago. They both loved the color red and playing soccer during recess. They both loved pickles but hated cucumbers. And they both *really* loved science. One day Pablo was going to fly a spaceship, just like the one on his shirt. Violet was going to discover cures for all kinds of diseases when she grew up.

"Hey, Violet! We got the same teacher again!" said Pablo.

"I know!" replied Violet. Her nose wiggled with excitement.

"You two have a great first day! And don't get into too much trouble." Pablo's mom winked.

"We won't!" Pablo and Violet replied.

They headed into their classroom. The desks were arranged in groups of three.

"Yes!" Violet cried. "We're sitting in the same group."

Pablo read the name tag on the third desk. "Deepak. Who is that?"

Violet shrugged.

DING, DING, DING! Their teacher rang the bell on his desk.

"Welcome, everyone. I'm Mr. Eng. I've planned a lot of fun activities this year."

Acknowledgments

I wouldn't be able to write this series were it not for the unconditional support of my partner, Jorge. Thank you for being one of my biggest fans. Mom, thank you for continually guiding me from above. I feel your presence always, and I miss you dearly. Dad, thank you for always supporting me in anything I do. And thank you for passing along your love of books and reading to me. You are the most wonderful Tata to Violeta and Lila. You mean the world to us. To my sweet, smart, and kind daughters, Violeta and Lila, time is moving entirely too fast. Everything I do is for you both, and I hope I make you proud. I am blessed to work with the talented Random House Children's Books team. Thank you,

Caroline Abbey, for giving me a shot. Thank you also to Tricia Lin, Jasmine Hodge, Lili Feinberg, Kimberly Small, and countless others, who have helped bring these books to life. You all have been tremendously supportive, and I am so lucky to be a part of such an amazing and hardworking team. Finally, I'd like to thank my marvelous agent, Chelsea Eberly. Thank you for your continued guidance and support!